Little Metis
and the
Metis Sash

Written by **Deborah L. Delaronde**

Illustrated by

Keiron Flamand

Dedicated to:

The Metis people, both past and present.

Family members worked together. Each member (child, parent, grandparent, etc.) had their own chores to do in order to help with the day-to-day preparation toward a common goal: food, clothing and warmth.

I hope this story serves as a reminder of the way life was and could be again. Despite the differences in our ages, families or cultural backgrounds, each of us has something unique that we can share with our family, friends and community.

Little Metis sat watching his Grandmother as she braided coloured rags together to make floor rugs.

"Everyone is always busy doing something. I'm sOOOoo bored. There's nothing to do!!" Little Metis said to his Grandmother.

"Can I help you with your rug, Kookum - Grandmother?" Little Metis asked hopefully.

"Well….. You can cut the rags in strips so that I can tie them into my braiding," Kookum said as she smiled at her grandson.

But when Little Metis had done what his Grandmother had asked him to do, he soon became bored.

"Do you think Shoomish - Grandfather needs my help?" he asked.

"Shoomish always likes you helping him. He's working by the lake. Why don't you go ask him…… but don't get lost," Grandmother warned him.

Little Metis stepped outside and saw different-ent colored spools of wool placed in a neat row on a wooden spool holder.

He had a GREAT IDEA so that he would not get lost.

He picked up the end of the BLUE WOOL and walked towards the lake. As he walked, a playful Noodin - Wind blew the wool high in the sky. He turned and laughed as he tugged on the blue wool, making braided patterns in the sky.

Little Metis found Shoomish by the lake smoking fish fillets as he cleaned his nets of Giingoo - Fish.

"Hi Shoomish. There's nothing for me to do….. can I help you?" he asked hopefully.

"Sure. You can gather more grass, twigs and wood so that I can keep the smoke going for the fish fillets," Grandfather said.

But little Metis wanted to fish so that he could catch and smoke his own fish….. just like his Grandfather. So….. he took the blue end of the wool, tied a hook on the end and threw it into the water. He then went back to gathering grass, twigs and wood for his Grandfather.

When he had done what Grandfather had asked him to do, he soon became bored again.

"Well…..," Little Metis sighed and said, "If there's nothing else to do, I think I'll go back to Kookum's."

He walked back to Kookum's, following the blue wool trail. Behind him, the frisky wind tugged on the wool and a huge fish flew out of the water and landed on the shore.

"Hi Kookum. There's NOTHING for me to do again. Do you think my Dad needs help?"

"Your Dad is in the bush and I'm sure he has something for you to do. Why don't you go and ask him….. but don't get lost."

Little Metis stepped outside….. picked up the end of the GREEN WOOL and walked towards the bush. As he walked, the playful wind blew the wool high in the sky. He turned and laughed as he tugged on the green wool, making fish patterns in the sky.

He found his Dad setting snares to catch Waboose - Rabbits.
"Hi Dad. There's nothing for me to do. Can I help you?" Little
Metis asked hopefully.

"Sure, you can cut pieces of wire for me," his Dad said, smiling
at him.

But Little Metis wanted to make his own snare for catching rabbits….. just like his Dad. So he wound his green wool into a circle on the branch of a tree.

He then sat down to cut wires for his Dad.

When he had done what his Dad had asked him to do, he soon became bored again.

"If you don't have anything else for me to do, I think I'll go back to Kookum's," he said to his Dad.

Little Metis walked back to Kookum's house by following the green wool trail. Behind him, the gentle wind picked up the wool and wrapped itself around the neck of a rabbit.

"Hi Kookum. I'm back and I'm bored again!! Do you think Akiwenzii - Old Man might need my help?"

"There must be something you can do for him. Go and ask him, but don't get lost."

Little Metis stepped outside….. grabbed the end of the GOLD WOOL and walked to Akiwenzii's cabin.

As he walked, the playful wind blew the wool high in the sky. He turned and laughed as he tugged on the gold wool, making rabbit patterns in the sky.

Little Metis found Akiwenzii making Bagwezhigan - Bannock. He was wrapping a piece of bannock around a stick to set it over the fire.

"Hi, Akiwenzii. There's nothing for me to do….. can I help you?" asked Little Metis hopefully.

"You can flour and knead the rest of the bannock while I go and cook my stew."

But Little Metis wanted to make bannock of his own….. just like Akiwenzii. So he took Akiwenzii's bannock and cut it into little pieces.

He then threaded his wool through each piece of dough and stretched them over the fire.

Little Metis sat and watched the bannock cooking over the fire, but soon became bored again.

He went to Akiwenzii's house and said, "If you don't have anything else for me to do, I think I'll go back to my Kookum's." He walked back to Kookum's house by following the gold wool trail.

Behind him, the wind was growing stronger. It picked up the golden string of bannocks and waved them in the air.

When Akiwenzii stepped outside to check on his bannock, he saw a string of flying bannocks! He ran and jumped up to catch them, but a puff of wind blew the bannock flour all over him.

"Kookum, I'm back again with NOTHING to do!!" Little Metis said. "Do you think Mom needs my help?"

"Sure, maybe she's already wishing you were there to help her. Go and ask her….. but don't get lost."

He walked outside…... grabbed the end of the RED WOOL and walked home.

As he walked, the gusty but playful wind blew the wool high in the sky. He turned and laughed as he tugged on the red wool, making bannock patterns in the sky.

Little Metis found his Mom pounding thin strips of dried buffalo meat on a hollowed-out rock. "Hi Mom. There's nothing to do….. can I help you?" Little Metis asked hopefully.

"Am I glad to see you!! You can grind the rest of this meat until it's a powder. I'll go and melt buffalo fat so that I can pour it over the meat to make Kas ke uk - Pemmican.

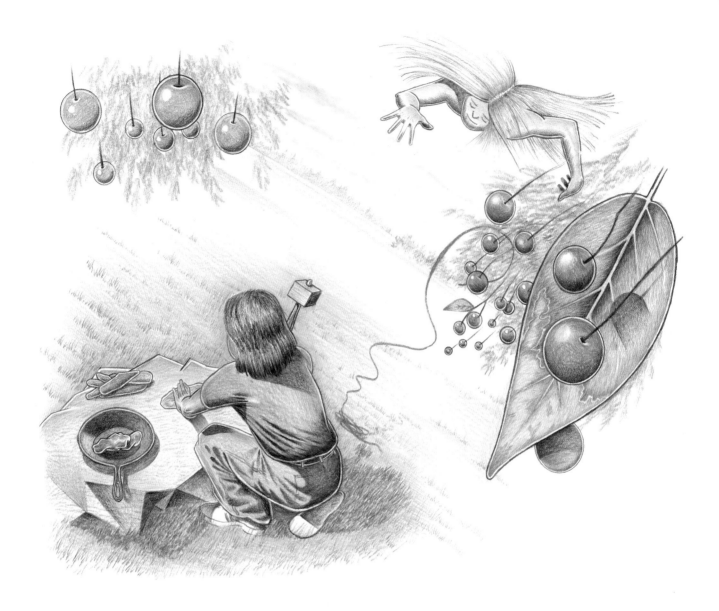

But Little Metis wanted to make pemmican….. just for him. He pounded on a small strip of buffalo meat to soften it, tied his red wool around the meat and tossed it into the pan of powdered meat. But the blustery wind picked up the red wool and wrapped it over the branch of a cranberry tree.

When Little Metis had done what his Mom had asked him to do, he became bored once again.

"I'm going back to Kookum's house," he shouted to his Mom.

He walked back to his Kookum's house by following the red wool trail. Behind him, the wind had grown ever stronger. It jerked the wool so hard that cranberries fell down from the tree and into the pan of powdered meat.

Little Metis' Mom came out with a pot of melted grease and poured it over the meat. When she looked down into the pan to begin stirring her pemmican, she saw that the meat had turned red. And….. what was a string of red wool doing in the pan? she thought.

When Little Metis arrived back at Kookum's cabin, he saw Grandpa dragging a Great Big Giingoo - Fish with the BLUE WOOL coming out of its mouth, and holding a ball of blue wool in his other hand.

Dad was walking beside a baby Waboose - Rabbit with the GREEN WOOL wrapped around its head as a collar, and a ball of green wool in his other hand.

Akiwenzii walking towards him with a string of
Bagwezhigan - Bannocks flying in the wind behind him and a ball
of gold wool in his other hand.

And his Mom walking towards them holding a big chunk of
Kas ke uk - Pemmican with the RED WOOL tied into it and a ball
of red wool in her other hand.

Everyone was upset with Little Metis because he had interrupted their work.

Kookum came out to see what the noise was all about.

"I don't have time for this, I have my work to do," Grandpa grumbled.

"What am I supposed to do with this baby rabbit?" Dad asked.

"I should get you to make bannock for me all week!" Akiwenzii demanded.

"My Pemmican is going to have a sour cranberry taste!" Mom complained.

Little Metis tried to explain to everyone what had happened.
"I was bored and I wanted to learn so I thought I would learn by helping everyone with their work," he said.

Kookum came to her grandson's side. "Little Metis was only trying to help all of you and I'm sure he did whatever you asked him to do," she told everyone.

"But, since we're all here now, I think we need to take a break, so why don't we stop our work and share a meal. I'm sure Little Metis can tell us what happened after we've eaten.

"Now… young man," she continued, "since you've been playing with my wool, take the WHITE WOOL… and get some vegetables from the garden for our supper. Don't get lost or into any trouble.

"And this time… please wind it up as you walk home," Grandma said, smiling.

Little Metis was glad to get away. He picked up the white string, walked through the trees to where Kookum planted her garden. The wind picked up the white wool, but a tree branch pulled it down and it slipped out of sight without him knowing that he had lost it.

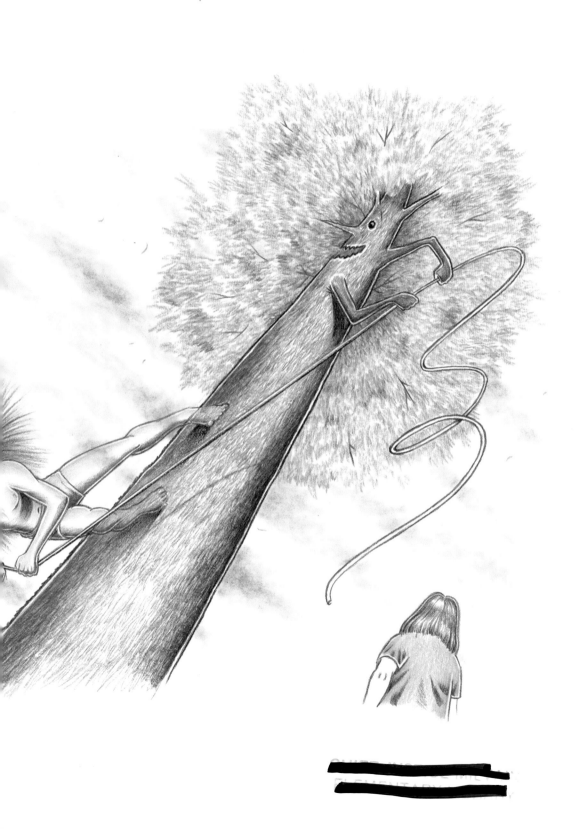

He dug around the potato plant, pulled up some carrots and tugged on some corn cobs. Little Metis' arms were full and when he looked around, he found that he was surrounded by trees.

"Huh?" he gasped. "Where's Grandma's house?? Where's my string? Oh no, I'm lost!!," he said fearfully.

Just then a forceful wind tore the white wool from the tree branch and it flew up into the air towards little Metis.

"Yipppyippee!!," he shouted and began walking towards the white wool. Little Metis looked up and saw that a Little Boy of Wind was bringing him the end of his white wool. He now knew that the Little Boy of Wind had been playing games with him all afternoon.

When Little Metis arrived back at Kookum's cabin, she cleaned the vegetables and used his fish to cook a pot of Giingoonhwaaboo - fish soup, but she also fried a piece of fish specially for him. Everyone was given a piece of Little Metis' flying bannock. And….. for dessert….. Kookum unwrapped a huge piece of Anishinaabe ziinzibaakwad - Maple Sugar Candy that she always saved for special occasions.

When everyone had finished eating, Kookum left the room for a minute and returned with a package. She handed the package to Little Metis.

The wind moaned and wailed as it pushed against the windows to get a peek.

"A present?" Little Metis shouted excitedly as he tore at the package and found….. a Metis Sash!

It was woven with all of the colours of wool that he had used so he wouldn't get lost.

"Little Metis," Kookum said, clearing her voice. "I wove this sash for you.

"You gathered the food and the people we needed to make this family meal possible.

"The Metis Sash is usually given to young Metis men when they begin hunting and gathering food for their families. You've done all of that today, so we think it's time you started to wear your very own Metis Sash.

"Sometimes we forget that everyone can help… even a little Metis," Kookum said, smiling proudly.

And from that day on, Little Metis could never say he was bored again!!

The Metis Sash

The original colours of the Metis Sash were: green/red/tan/brown. Metis men wore the Sash daily due to its many uses that contributed to their survival in the bush. The tassels could be used to repair snowshoes, dog harnesses and bridles. The foot-long tassels could not only be used to make snares, but could also be used to repair torn clothing while out in the bush. More importantly, it was wrapped around the waist to hold the heat in to the upper part of the body.

It was also used to carry canoes or heavy sacks strapped across the back. The Metis Sash (cienture fleche or arrow sash) was originally woven entirely by hand and could be anywhere from 12 to 16 feet. It took anywhere from 60 to 100 hours to finger weave a Metis Sash.

The colours seen in Metis Sashes today are green/red/blue/gold/white. Today, the Metis Sash is worn when attending special occasions.

Modern Metis Sashes are woven on a four-harness loom or on an Inkle loom. The traditional arrow pattern is still used, and the coloured sashes have become a symbol of the Metis Nation.

To the Metis, the Order of the Sash parallels the Order of Canada.

Glossary

Special Thanks to **Rita Flamand** for her Saulteaux Translation.

Ojibway	English
Kookum	Grandmother
Shoomish	Grandfather
Giingoo	Fish
Waboose	Rabbit
Akiwenzii	Old Man
Bagwezhigan	Bannock or Bread
Kas ke uk	Pemmican
Noodin	Wind
Giingoonh waa boo	Fish Soup

Anishinabe	
Ziinzbaakwad	Maple Sugar Candy

Deborah Delaronde - *Author*

Deborah Delaronde (Metis) lives and works in the community of Duck Bay, Manitoba. **Little Metis and the Metis Sash** is Deborah's second book. Her first book, **A Name for a Metis**, was published in 1999. Deborah writes Metis stories for Metis children. Few books exist that are written by the Metis for the Metis. Deborah also enjoys sharing her stories with others.

Keiron Flamand - *Illustrator*

Keiron Flamand (Metis) lives in the Metis community of Camperville, Manitoba. Keiron is a freelance artist and has illustrated several of Pemmican's books, including **A Name for a Metis** and **How Lone Crow Became Magpie**. Keiron is also a writer, and his book, **Buffalo and Sprucegum**, was one of Pemmican's early publications.